Irish
Fairytales

Irish Fairytales

Sixteen enchanting myths and
legends from the emerald isle

RETOLD BY PHILIP WILSON

ILLUSTRATED BY
SUE CLARKE, ANNA CYNTHIA LEPLAR, JACQUELINE MAIR,
SHELIA MOXLEY, AND JANE TATTERSFIELD

ARMADILLO

Contents

Introduction

The Irish have an inexhaustible hunger for folk and fairytales – tales of wonder, magic, and mystery. The stories in this book are just a few of the thousands such tales that have been written down, by individual folklorists in the nineteenth century and by the collectors of the Irish Folklore Commission and its successors in the twentieth. But these thousands of tales are just a sample of the millions that have been told by word of mouth beside the fire for years uncounted.

A fairy tale is a living thing, and it is most alive when springing from the mouth of a storyteller. So these are stories to read, but also to tell and retell.

Of course not all fairytales were told round the fireside. Stories could be told anywhere and everywhere. Thomas Crofton Croker, who recorded "The Story of the Little Bird", left an account of how he learned it from an old woman at a religious meeting held at a holy well dedicated to a patron saint. He writes, "It was a beautiful summer evening, and, weary with walking, I had sat down to rest upon a grassy bank, close to a holy well. I felt refreshed at the sight of the clear cold water, through which pebbles glistened, and sparks of silvery air shot upwards: in short, I was in a temper to be pleased. An old woman had concluded her prayers, and was about to depart, when I entered into conversation with her, and I have written the very words in which she related to me the legend of the "Song of the Little Bird."

There is something deeply, intrinsically Irish about "The Story of the Little Bird", and the sudden ageing of the monk recalls the fate of the Irish hero Oisín when he returns from the Land of Youth. Yet, as with all the other stories in this book, parallels can be found in many cultures. Folklorists call this particular tale type "The Monk and the Bird". It appears in a French sermon of the twelfth century, and versions have been recorded all over – in Estonia, Greece, China, even in Mexico.

This diffusion of the same storylines right across the world claims the fairy tale as part of the common human heritage. But it also true that tales naturalise like flowers in a particular culture, so that it is just as true to say that the stories in this book are strongly Irish, as to say that similar stories can be found elsewhere. Such stories belong to the world, to a particular culture, and to each individual storyteller. The storyteller re-shapes the story with every telling, adding grace notes of individual creativity.

Storytellers were very highly regarded in Irish society, and some of them had an enormous store of tales. The stories of one such traditional storyteller, Seán Ó Conaill, fill a fat book, and the man who recorded his repertoire, Séamus Ó Duilearga, described him as "a conscious literary artist" rather than a passive tradition-bearer. Ó Conaill himself said, "Many though the tales be which I have told to you, I have forgotten as much again; that I assure you is the truth."

Folklorist Tadhg Ó Murchú vividly conveys the way in which traditional storytelling did not depend simply on words, either memorised or improvised, but on performance techniques. Describing one Kerry storyteller, he writes: "His piercing eyes are on my face, his limbs are trembling, as, immersed in his story, and forgetful of all else, he puts his very soul into the telling. Obviously much affected by his narrative, he uses a great deal of gesticulation, and, by the movement of his body, hands, and head, tries to convey hate and anger, fear and humour, like an actor in a play."

Irish fairytales are suffused with poetry and also shot through with humour. Philip Wilson's choice of stories in this volume, and his skilful retelling of them, gives a good flavour of the kinds of stories told in Ireland. They range from the eerie story of "The Horned Women" (a tale which, like "The Demon Cat", was first published by Oscar Wilde's mother), to the comic antics of "Hudden and Dudden and Donald O'Neary" or Fin in "The Giant's Causeway", to narratives of great beauty and mystery such as "The Story of Deirdre" or "Fair, Brown, and Trembling."

"Fair, Brown, and Trembling" is a Cinderella story. As often in Catholic countries, the Cinderella-figure, Trembling, makes three visits to church, rather than to a ball. As sometimes happens, the story goes on beyond Trembling's marriage to the prince, with another magical adventure. The tragic tale of doomed love in "The Story of Deirdre" is one of the "Three Most Sorrowful Tales of Erin", and it was first written down in the twelfth-century Book of Leinster.

The poet W. B. Yeats, who compiled two collections of Irish fairytales, described them as "the simplest and most unforgettable thoughts of the generations". Since Yeats, many other books of Irish fairytales have appeared, of which I particularly recommend Sean O'Sullivan's *Folktales of Ireland* and Henry Glassie's *Irish Folk Tales*.

"There now is the story for you, from the first word to the last, as I heard it from my grandmother."

NEIL PHILIP

The Leprechaun's Gold

It was Lady Day and everyone who had worked on the harvest had a holiday. The sun shone brightly, and there was a pleasant breeze, so Tom Fitzpatrick decided to go for a walk across the fields. He had been strolling for a while, when he heard a high-pitched noise, "Clickety-click, clickety-click," like the sound of a small bird chirruping.

Tom wondered what creature could be making this noise, so he crept quietly towards the sound. As he peered through some bushes, the noise stopped suddenly, and what did Tom see but a tiny old man,

with a leather apron, sitting on a little wooden stool. Next to the old man was a large brown jar. The little man seemed to be repairing a miniature shoe, just large enough for his own feet. Tom could not believe what he saw.

All the stories Tom had heard about the fantastic riches of the little people came back into his mind. "If I'm careful," he said to himself, "I've got it made." And Tom remembered that you should never take your eyes away from one of the little people, otherwise they disappear.

"Good day to you," said Tom. "Would you mind telling me what's in your jar?"

"Beer, some of the best there is," said the little man.

"And where did you get it from?"

"I made it myself. You'll never guess what I made it from."

"I suppose you made it from malt," said Tom.

"Wrong!" said the leprechaun. "I made it from heather!"

"You never did! You can't make beer from heather!"

"Don't you know about the Vikings? When they were here in Ireland they told my ancestors how to make beer from heather, and the secret has been in my family ever since. But you shouldn't be wasting time asking me pointless questions. Look over there where the cows have broken into the corn field and are trampling all over the corn."

Tom started to turn round, but remembered just in time that it was a trick to make him look away from the little man. He lunged at the leprechaun, knocking over the jar of beer, and grasped the little man in his hand. Tom was angry at being tricked, and was sad to have knocked over the beer, which he had wanted to taste. But he had the creature safe in his hand.

"That's enough of your tricks!" shouted Tom.

"Show me where you keep your gold, or I'll squeeze the life out of you before you can blink!"

And Tom put on such a fearsome expression that the leprechaun began to quake with fright, and to worry that Tom might truly hurt him. So he said to Tom, "You just carry me through the next couple of fields, and I'll show you the biggest crock of gold you could imagine."

So off they went. Tom held the leprechaun tightly in his fist, so that, no matter how much he wriggled and slithered, the little man could not escape. And Tom looked straight at the tiny creature, never changing his gaze, so that the leprechaun had no chance to disappear.

They walked on and on, over fields, across ditches, and through hedges. They even had to cross a crooked patch of bog, but somehow Tom managed to get through it without once looking away from the leprechaun. Finally they arrived at a field that was full of hundreds and hundreds of turnips. The leprechaun told Tom to walk towards the middle of the field, where he pointed towards a large turnip. "You just dig under that one," said the leprechaun, "and you'll find a crock full to the brim with gold coins."

Tom had nothing to dig with. He realised that he would have to go home and get his spade. But how would he find the right turnip when he returned? Quickly, he bent down to remove one of the red ribbons

holding up his gaiters, and tied the ribbon around the turnip. "Now you swear to me," he said to the little creature, "that you won't take the ribbon from that turnip before I return."

The leprechaun swore that he would not remove the ribbon, and Tom ran home to get his spade. He ran as fast as he could, because he could not wait to unearth the leprechaun's gold.

By the time Tom ran back to the turnip field, he was quite breathless. But when he opened the gate into the field he could not believe his eyes. Across the entire field a mass of red ribbons was blowing in the breeze. The leprechaun had kept his promise. He had not taken away Tom's ribbon. Instead he had tied an identical ribbon to every single turnip in the field. Now Tom knew he would never find the leprechaun's gold. His dream of fabulous riches was over.

Tom walked sulkily back home, cursing the leprechaun as he went. And every time he passed a turnip field, he gave one of the turnips a mighty wallop with his spade.

The Horned Women

It happened five hundred or more years ago, when all well-to-do women learned how to prepare and card their wool and spin it to make yarn. One evening, a rich lady sat up late in her chamber, carding a new batch of wool. The rest of the family and all the servants had gone to bed, and the house was silent. Suddenly, the lady heard a loud knocking at the door, together with a loud, high-pitched voice shouting "Open the door! Open the door!".

The lady of the house, who did not recognise the voice, was puzzled.

"Who is it?" she called.

"I am the Witch of One Horn," came the reply.

The lady, who could not hear clearly through the thick oak door, thought that it was one of her neighbours who needed help, or one of the servants in a panic, so she rushed across the room and threw open the door. The lady was quite astonished to see a tall woman, with a single horn growing in the middle of her head. The newcomer, who was carrying a pair of carders, strode across the room, sat down, and set to work carding some of the lady's wool. She worked in silence, but all of a sudden, she looked around the room and said, "Where are the others? They should be here by now."

Straight away, there was another knock on the door.

Although she was by now rather frightened, the lady of the house could not stop herself from crossing the room and opening the door once more. To her surprise another witch came into the room, this time with a pair of horns and carrying a spinning wheel.

"Make room for me," she said. "I am the Witch of Two Horns." And no sooner had she said this than she started to spin, producing fine woollen yarn faster than anyone the lady had seen before.

Again and again, there came knocks on the door, and again and again the lady felt she had to get and up and let in the newcomers. This went on until there were twelve women in the room, and each had one horn more than the previous witch. They all sat around the fire, carding and spinning and weaving, and the lady of the house did not know what to do. She wanted to get up and run away, but her legs would not let her; she wanted to scream for help, but her mouth would not open. She began to realise that she was under the spell of the horned women.

As she sat watching them, wondering what she could do, one of the witches called to her: "Don't just sit there. Get up and bake us all a cake."

Suddenly, the lady found she could stand up. She looked around for a pot to take to the well to get some water for the cake mixture, but there was nothing that she could use. One of the hags saw her looking and said to her, "Here, take this sieve and collect some water in that."

The lady knew that a sieve could not hold water, but the witches' spell made her powerless to do anything else but walk off to the well and try to fill the sieve. As the water poured through the sieve, the lady sat down and cried.

Through her sobs, the lady heard a voice. It seemed as if the spirit of the well was talking to her. "There is some clay and moss behind the well-shaft. Take them, mix them together,

and make a lining for the sieve. Then it will hold water."

The lady did as she was told, and the voice spoke again. "Go back to the house, and when you come to the corner, scream three times and shout these words as loud as you can: 'The mountain of the Fenian women is all aflame.'"

Straight away the lady's screams were echoed by the cries of the horned women. All twelve witches dashed out of the house and flew away at high speed to their mountain, Slievenamon, and the lady was released from the spell. She sighed a huge sigh of relief, but she saw quickly that the witches had made their own cake and poisoned the rest of her family. The lady turned to the well, asking the spirit "How can I help my children and servants? And what shall I do if they return here again?"

So the spirit of the well taught the lady how to protect herself if the witches should return. First she had to sprinkle on her threshold some water in which she had washed her child's feet. Next she was to take pieces of the witches' cake and place a piece in the mouth of each member of her household, to bring them back to life. Then the spirit told her to take the cloth woven by the witches, and put it into her chest. And finally she was to place a heavy oak crossbeam across the door. The lady did all these things, and waited.

Soon the twelve witches returned, screaming and howling, for they had arrived at their mountain and found no fire, and were mad for vengeance.

"Open the door! Open, foot-water!" they yelled, and their cries made people tremble in the next village.

"I cannot open," called the water, "I am all scattered on the ground."

"Open the door! Open wood and beam!" they shouted, and their noise could be heard far over the hills.

"I cannot open," said the door. "For I am fastened with a stout crossbeam."

"Open the door! Open cake that we made with our enemies' blood!" they screamed, and their screams could be heard by the sea.

"I cannot open," said the cake. "For I am broken in pieces."

And then the witches knew that they were defeated, and flew back to their mountain, cursing the spirit of the well as they went.

The lady of the house was finally left in peace. When she went outside to see that the coast was clear, she found a cloak that one of the witches had dropped. She hung the cloak up in her room, and it was kept in her family for five hundred years, in memory of her victory over the twelve horned women.

Hudden and Dudden and Donald O'Neary

Once upon a time there were two farmers, called Hudden and Dudden. They each had a huge farm, with lush pastures by the river for their herds of cows, and hillside fields for their sheep. Their beasts always brought good prices at the market. But no matter how well they did, they always wanted more.

Between Hudden's and Dudden's land was a little field with a tiny old cottage in the middle, and in this house lived a poor man named Donald O'Neary. Donald only had one cow, called Daisy, and barely enough grass to feed her.

Although he was only poor and had but a narrow strip of farmland, Hudden and Dudden were jealous of Donald. They wanted to turf him out and divide his land between them, so that they could make their farms even bigger. And whenever the two rich farmers met up, their talk would always turn to how they could get rid of poor Donald.

One day, they were talking about this and Hudden suddenly said, "Let's kill Daisy. If he has no cow, he'll soon clear out." So, Hudden and Dudden crept quietly into Donald's cow-shed, fed some poison to Daisy, and made off with all speed.

At nightfall, Donald went to the shed to check that Daisy was comfortable. The cow turned to her master, licked his hand affectionately, collapsed on to the floor, and died.

Donald was saddened at Daisy's death. But, because he was a poor fellow, he had learned long ago how to cope with hardship, and he soon began to think whether he could turn his misfortune to good use. "At least I can get some money for Daisy's hide," he thought. And then he had an idea.

The next day, Donald marched off to the fair in the nearby town, with the hide slung over his shoulder. Before he got to the fair, he stopped in a quiet spot, made some slits in the hide, and put a penny in each of the slits. Then he chose the town's best inn, strode through the door, hung up the hide on a nail, and ordered a glass of the best whisky.

The landlord looked suspiciously at Donald's ragged clothes. "Don't worry that I can't pay you," said Donald. "I may look poor, but this hide gives me all the money I want." Donald walked over to the hide, hit it with his stick, and out fell a penny. The landlord was flabbergasted.

"What can I give you for that hide?" he asked.

"It's not for sale," replied Donald. "Me and my family have lived off that hide for years. I'm not going to sell it now." And Donald whacked the hide again, producing another penny.

Eventually, after the hide had produced several more pennies, the landlord could stand it no longer. "I'll give you a whole bag of gold for that hide!" he shouted. Donald, who could not believe his good fortune, gave in, and the deal was struck.

When Donald got home, he called on his neighbour Hudden. "Would you lend me your scales? I sold a hide at the fair today and want to work out how much I have made."

Hudden could not believe his eyes as Donald tipped the gold into his scales. "You got all that for one hide?" he asked. And as soon as Donald had gone home, he raced round to Dudden's, to tell him what had happened. Dudden could not believe that poor Donald had sold Daisy's hide for a whole bagful of gold, so Hudden took his neighbour to Donald's hovel, so that he could see for himself. They walked straight into Donald's cottage without knocking on the door, and there was Donald sitting at the table, counting his gold.

"Good evening Hudden; good evening Dudden. You thought you were so clever, playing your tricks on me. But you did me a good turn. I took

Daisy's skin to the fair, where hides are fetching their weight in gold."

The next day, Hudden and Dudden slaughtered all their cattle, every single cow and calf in their fine herds. They loaded the hides on to Hudden's cart and set off to the fair.

When they arrived, Hudden and Dudden each took one of the largest hides, and walked up and down the market square shouting "Fine hides! Fine hides! Who'll buy our fine hides?" Soon a tanner went up to Hudden and Dudden.

"How much are you charging for your hides?"

"Just their weight in gold."

"You must have been in the tavern all morning if you think I'll fall for that one," said the tanner, shaking his head.

Then a cobbler came up to them.

"How much are you charging for your hides?"

"Just their weight in gold."

"What sort of a fool do you take me for?" shouted the cobbler, and

landed Hudden a punch in the belly that made him stagger backwards. People heard this commotion and came running from all over the fair ground. One of the crowd was the innkeeper. "What's going on?" he shouted.

"A pair of villains trying to sell hides for their weight in gold," replied the cobbler.

"Grab them! They're probably friends of the con-man who cheated me out of a bag of gold pieces yesterday," said the innkeeper. But Hudden and Dudden took to their heels. They got a few more punches, and some nips from the dogs of the town, and some tears in their clothes, but the innkeeper did not catch them, and eventually they ran all the way home.

Donald O'Neary saw them coming, and could not resist laughing at them. But Hudden and Dudden were not laughing. They were determined to punish Donald. Before the poor man knew what was happening, Hudden had grabbed a sack, and Dudden had forced Donald into it and tied up the opening. "We'll carry him off to the Brown Lake and throw him in!" said Dudden.

But Hudden and Dudden were tired, with running from the town and carrying Donald, so they stopped for a drink on the way, leaving Donald, in his sack, on the inn doorstep.

Once more, Donald began to think how he could gain from his problem, and he started to scream and shout inside the sack: "I won't have her. I won't have her I tell you!" He repeated this on and on until a

farmer, who had just arrived with a drove of cattle, took notice.

"What do you mean?" asked the farmer.

"The king's daughter. They are forcing me to marry the king's daughter, but I won't have her."

The farmer thought how fine it would be to marry the king's daughter, to be dressed in velvet and jewels, and never again to get up at dawn to milk the cows.

"I'll swap places with you," said the farmer. "You can take my herd, and I will get into the sack and be taken to marry the king's daughter."

So the farmer untied the sack and let out Donald O'Neary. "Don't mind the shaking on the way, it will be just the steep palace steps. And don't worry if they curse you or call you a rogue. They are angry because I have been shouting that I don't want to marry the princess." said Donald.

Quickly, the farmer got into the sack, and Donald tied up the cord and drove away the herd of cattle. He was long gone when Hudden and Dudden came out of the inn and picked up their burden. Refreshed

with their whisky, they soon arrived at the lake, threw in the sack, and returned home.

Hudden and Dudden could not believe their eyes when they arrived. There was Donald O'Neary, as large as life, with a large new herd of fine fat cattle.

Donald said, "There's lots of fine cattle down at the bottom of the lake.

Why shouldn't I take some for myself? Come along with me and I will show you." When they got to the lake, Donald pointed to the reflections of the clouds in the water. "Don't you see the cattle?" he said. Greedy to own a rich herd like their neighbour, the two farmers dived headfirst into the waters of the lake. And they have never been seen since.

Munachar and Manachar

There were once two little fellows called Munachar and Manachar. They liked to pick raspberries, but Manachar always ate them all. Munachar got so fed up with this that he said he would look for a rod to make a gibbet to hang Manachar.

Soon, Munachar came to a rod. "What do you want?" said the rod. "A rod, to make a gibbet," replied Munachar.

"You won't get me," said the rod, "unless you can get an axe to cut me." So Munachar went to find an axe. "What do you want?" said the

axe. "I am looking for an axe, to cut a rod, to make a gibbet," replied Munachar.

"You won't get me," said the axe, "unless you can get a stone to sharpen me." So Munachar went to find a stone. "What do you want?" said the stone. "I am looking for a stone, to sharpen an axe, to cut a rod, to make a gibbet," replied Munachar.

"You won't get me," said the stone, "unless you can get water to wet me." So Munachar went to find water. "What do you want?" said the water. "I am looking for water to wet a stone, to sharpen an axe, to cut a rod, to make a gibbet," replied Munachar.

"You won't get me," said the water, "unless you can get a deer who will swim me." So Munachar went to look for a deer.

"What do you want?" said the deer. "I am looking for a deer, to swim some water, to wet a stone, to sharpen an axe, to cut a rod, to make a gibbet," replied Munachar.

"You won't get me," said the deer, "unless you can get a hound who will hunt me." So Munachar went to look for a hound. "What do you want?" said the hound. "I am looking for a hound, to hunt a deer, to swim some water, to wet a stone, to sharpen an axe, to cut a rod, to make a gibbet," replied Munachar.

"You won't get me," said the hound, "unless you can get a piece of butter to put in my claw." So Munachar went to look for some butter.

"What do you want?" said the butter. "I am looking for a piece of butter to put in the claw of a hound, to hunt a deer, to swim some water, to wet a stone, to sharpen an axe, to cut a rod, to make a gibbet," replied Munachar.

"You won't get me," said the butter, "unless you can get a cat who can scrape me." So Munachar went to look for a cat.

"What do you want?" said the cat. "I am looking for a cat to scrape some butter, to put in the claw of a hound, to hunt a deer, to swim some water, to wet a stone, to sharpen an axe, to cut a rod, to make a gibbet," replied Munachar.

"You won't get me," said the cat, "unless you can get some milk to feed me." So Munachar went to get some milk. "What do you want?" said the milk. "I am looking for some milk, to feed a cat, to scrape some butter, to put in the claw of a hound, to hunt a deer, to swim some water, to wet a stone, to sharpen an axe, to cut a rod, to make a gibbet," replied Munachar.

"You won't get me," said the milk, "unless you can bring me some straw from those threshers over there." So Munachar went to ask the threshers. "What do you want?" said the threshers. "I am looking for some straw, to give to the milk, to feed a cat, to scrape some butter, to put in the claw of a hound, to hunt a deer, to swim some water, to wet a stone, to sharpen an axe, to cut a rod, to make a gibbet," replied Munachar.

"You won't get any straw," said the threshers, "unless you bring some flour to bake a cake from the miller next door." So Munachar went to ask the miller. "What do you want?" said the miller. "I am looking for some flour to bake a cake, to give to the threshers, to get some straw, to give to the milk, to feed a cat, to scrape some butter, to put in the claw of a hound, to hunt a deer, to swim some water, to wet a stone, to sharpen an axe, to cut a rod, to make a gibbet," replied Munachar.

"You'll get no flour," said the miller, "unless you fill this sieve with water." Some crows flew over crying "Daub! Daub!" So Munachar daubed some clay on the sieve, so it would hold water.

And he took the water to the miller, who gave him the flour; he gave the flour to the threshers, who gave him some straw; he took the straw to the cow, who gave him some milk; he took the milk to the cat, who scraped some butter; he gave the butter to the hound, who hunted the deer; the deer swam the water; the water wet the stone; the stone sharpened the axe; the axe cut the rod; the rod made a gibbet – and when Munachar was ready to hang Manachar, he found that Manachar had BURST!

King O'Toole and his Goose

Many years ago lived a king called O'Toole. He was a great king, with a large and prosperous kingdom, and he loved to ride the length and breadth of his realm, through the woods and across the fields, hunting deer.

But as time went by the king grew old and infirm, and he could no longer ride and hunt. He became sad and bored, and did not know what to do. Then one day he saw a flock of geese flying across the sky. O'Toole admired the birds' graceful flight, and decided that he would buy his own goose, to amuse himself. The king loved to watch the goose flying around his lake, and every Friday, the bird dived into the water and caught a trout for O'Toole to eat.

The graceful flight of the goose, and the tasty fish she caught, made O'Toole happy. But one day the goose grew old like her master, and could no longer amuse the king or catch fish for him. Once more O'Toole became sad, and even thought of drowning himself in his own lake.

Then O'Toole was out walking and he saw a young man he had not met before.

"God save you, King O'Toole," said the young man.

"Good day to you," said the king. "I am King O'Toole, ruler of these parts, but how did you know my name?"

"Oh, never mind," said Saint Kavin, for it was he. "I know more than that. How is your goose today?"

"But however did you know about my goose?" said the king. "Oh, never mind," was the reply, "I must have heard about it somewhere."

King O'Toole was fascinated that a total stranger should know so much about him, so he started to talk with the young man. Eventually, O'Toole asked Saint Kavin what he did for a living.

"I make old things as good as new," said Saint Kavin.

"So are you some sort of tinker or magician?" asked O'Toole.

"No, my trade is better than those. What would you think if I made your old goose as good as new?"

At this, the king's eyes nearly popped out of his head. He whistled loudly and the goose came waddling slowly up to her master. It seemed impossible that the young man would be able to restore the crippled creature to health.

Saint Kavin looked at the goose. "I can help her," he said. "But I don't work for nothing. What will you give me if I can make her fly again?"

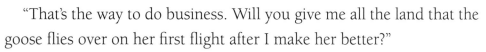

The king looked around him, thinking of the great lands and riches of his kingdom, and looked at the poor old goose. He wanted nothing more in the world than to see this creature hale and hearty once more. Even his kingdom seemed paltry by comparison. "I will give you anything that you ask for," replied King O'Toole.

"That's the way to do business. Will you give me all the land that the goose flies over on her first flight after I make her better?"

"I will," said the king. "Then it's a bargain," said Saint Kavin.

And with that, the saint beckoned, and the goose waddled heavily towards him, and looked up to his face, as if she was asking him what he would do next. Saint Kavin picked up the goose by her two wings, and made the sign of the cross on her back. Then he threw her into the air, saying "Whoosh!", as if he was producing a gust of wind to help her up into the sky. As soon as Saint Kavin had thrown her up, the goose soared up into the air, beat her wings gently, and was flying, high and fast, just as she had when the king first saw her.

King O'Toole could not believe his eyes. He stared up into the sky, with his mouth open in amazement, his eyes following every beat of the goose's wings and every turn of her flight. She seemed to be flying further, and higher, and more gracefully than ever before. Then the goose made a final turn and swooped down, to land at the king's feet, where he patted her gently on the head.

"And what do you say to me," said Saint Kavin, "for making her fly again?"

"It goes to show that nothing beats the art of man," said O'Toole.

"Anything else?" said Saint Kavin.

"And that I am beholden to you."

"But remember your promise," went on Saint Kavin. "Will you give me every patch of ground, every field and every forest, that she has flown over on her first flight?"

King O'Toole paused and looked at the young man. "Yes, I will," he said. "Even though she has flown over every acre of my kingdom. Even if I lose all my lands."

"That is well spoken, King O'Toole," said the young man.

"For your goose would not have flown again if you had gone back on your word."

So the king showed the young man all the lands of which he was now master. He called his scribes to draw up documents to prove that the kingdom had been passed from one man to the other. And so it was that Saint Kavin made himself known at last to King O'Toole. "I am Saint Kavin in disguise. I have done all this to test you, and you have not failed the test. You have done well, King O'Toole, and I will support you and give you food, drink, and somewhere to live now that you have given up your kingdom."

"Do you mean all this time I have been talking to the greatest of the saints, while I just took you for a young lad?" said the flabbergasted O'Toole.

"You know the difference now," replied Kavin.

And Saint Kavin was good as his word, and looked after O'Toole in his old age. But neither the king nor the goose lived long. The goose was killed by an eel when she was diving for trout, and the old king perished soon afterwards. He refused to eat his dead goose, for he said that he would not eat what Saint Kavin had touched with his holy hands.

The Story of Deirdre

Long ago in Ireland lived a man by the name of Malcolm Harper. He was a good man, with a wife, and a house, and lands of his own, but no family. One day, a soothsayer called on Malcolm, and when Malcolm found out that his visitor could see into the future, he asked if the soothsayer could foretell what the future held in store for him. The soothsayer paused, went out of the house for a few minutes to collect his thoughts and look into the future, and returned to face Malcolm.

"When I looked into the future I saw that you will have a daughter who will bring great trouble to many men in Ireland. Much blood will be spilled on her account, and three of the country's bravest heroes will lose their lives because of her."

A few years later a fine daughter was born to Malcolm's wife, and they called the girl Deirdre. Malcolm and his wife were afraid of the trouble she might bring them, so they decided to find a foster mother, who would agree to keep Deirdre away from the sight of men.

When they found a suitable foster-mother, they went to a far country and raised a mound of earth, and built inside a house, which could hardly be seen from outside. And there Deirdre and her foster-mother lived, unknown to the world, until the girl was sixteen years of age.

The foster-mother passed on all her knowledge to Deirdre, so soon the girl could sew and spin and cook, and knew all about the plants and flowers that grew around their hidden home.

Then one foul night, when a gale was blowing and black clouds filled the sky, a hunter passed the mound where Deirdre lived. He had lost the scent of his quarry, and found himself far away from his companions. Tired and lost, he settled down by the side of the grassy hillock to rest, and soon, with his tiredness and the oncoming dark, he fell into a deep sleep. As he slept, the hunter dreamed that he had come upon a place where the fairies lived. It seemed that he could hear the little creatures playing their music, and he began to shout out loud, "Let me in! I am a hunter far from home, and I need warmth and shelter."

Snug inside her house, Deirdre heard the huntsman's cry. "What noise is that? It sounds as if some poor creature needs our help."

Deirdre's foster-mother realised what they had heard, and tried to keep her ward away from the man outside. "Just some bird or beast looking for its mate," she replied. "Leave well alone, and it will disappear into the woods."

But Deirdre had heard the hunter asking to be let in, and, kind-hearted as she was, she would not turn away a creature in peril. "Foster-mother, you have taught me to be kind and considerate to others. I will

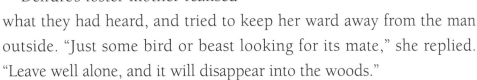

let the poor creature in and give it shelter." And Deirdre unbolted the door to their house, and let the hunter come in.

When the hunter saw Deirdre, he realised that there were many men at King Connachar's court who would be overwhelmed by her beauty. He mentioned especially the great hero, Naois, son of Uisnech, who would be glad of such a wife. Although Deirdre's foster-mother tried to persuade the hunter to tell no-one about the girl, he would make no such promise, and soon left, heading towards the royal palace.

As soon as he arrived at the court, he asked leave to speak to the king. "What is it you want?" asked Connachar.

"I came to tell you about the fairest woman I ever saw," replied the hunter. "Surely she must be the most beautiful in all of Ireland."

The king questioned the hunter about Deirdre, and promised him rich rewards if he would tell the king how to find her dwelling-place. Then King Connachar called for his kinsmen, and they rode off to find the place where Deirdre lived. When the king knocked at the door, the foster-mother, little thinking who it was, called out that she would only open if the king commanded her.

"This is King Connachar himself," he called, and they could do nothing but obey his command and open the door. As soon as Connachar saw Deirdre he wanted to carry her away and marry her forthwith. But Deirdre hesitated, asking the king to wait for a year and a day before their marriage. Connachar said he would wait, so long as she promised solemnly that she would marry him at the end of that time. Deirdre promised, and Connachar took her to his palace, where there were ladies-in-waiting to look after her every wish.

One day, Deirdre was out walking with her ladies, when a group of men came past. When she saw them, Deirdre was struck with their handsome appearance, and thought that they must be Naois, son of Uisnech, and his two brothers. Deirdre could not take her eyes from Naois as he passed, and realised that she was falling in love with the young lord. Suddenly, she gathered her gown about her and began to run after the young men, leaving her ladies-in-waiting behind. "Naois, son of Uisnech," she called. "Will you leave me behind?"

When he heard Deirdre calling, Naois turned back, saw the girl, and was smitten with love himself. Swiftly, he decided to take the girl with him, and they rode away together, Naois' brothers with them, never stopping until they reached Scotland.

Naois and his brothers Allen and Arden lived in their tower, and Deirdre was happy with them, until the time came when Deirdre had promised to marry Connachar. The king began to think how he might get Deirdre back, and he decided on this plan. He would hold a great feast, inviting all the lords from his kingdom and thereabouts, including Naois and his brothers. And Connachar sent his uncle, Ferchar Mac Ro, together with Ferchar's three sons, to Scotland, to invite Naois.

Deirdre was worried when she heard Ferchar tell Naois about the king's invitation. "Do not go," she begged. "It is a trick. I had a dream, in which I saw three hawks coming to Scotland and hovering above your tower. Their beaks were stained with red blood. They were coming for you."

But Naois insisted. "It will be bad luck for us if we do not accept the king's invitation," he said. And Ferchar Mac Ro agreed, saying, "If the king is kind to you, be kind to him in return. But if he is violent towards you, treat him in the same way. I and my three strong sons will stand by you." So Ferchar and his sons returned with Naois and his brothers. And although she was unwilling, and wept and trembled with fear, Deirdre went with them.

Once they had arrived at the palace of Connachar, Ferchar sent a message that he was back, and that Naois, Allen, Arden, and Deirdre were with him. Connachar was surprised, since he had thought that Naois would not have dared return. Because he was not yet ready to receive his guests, Connachar asked his servants to show them to a small house he kept for visitors, some way from the palace.

Connachar grew very impatient and anxious about Deirdre, so he sent his kinsman Gelban Grednach down to the house to see how they fared. "Tell me whether Deirdre looks well, and whether she is still as beautiful as she was," he ordered. Gelban crept down to the house and looked in at the spy hole in the door. There was Deirdre, together with Naois and his brothers, who were playing dice. Deirdre blushed, as she always did when someone looked at her, and Naois noticed her reddening face at once. Naois, maddened that someone should be spying on Deirdre, grabbed one of the dice and hurled it straight at the spy hole. Gelban reeled back in pain. The dice had taken out his eye. He scrambled back to the king, his hand clasped to his bleeding face.

Gelban told the king what had happened, adding that Deirdre was so beautiful he almost risked losing the sight in his other eye.

Connachar realised that he should lose no time, if Naois would ruin the sight of any man who even looked at Deirdre. So straight away he gathered together his three hundred bravest men, and they vowed to take Deirdre and kill her captors.

When Connachar and his men arrived, Ferchar's sons came to the aid of Naois, as they had promised. Never before was there such a fearsome sight, as the sons of Ferchar fought all comers, slashing left and right

with their swords, and killing every one of Connachar's men. The king could hardly control his wrath as Naois, his brothers, and Deirdre made their escape, and the sons of Ferchar left to tell their father all about their great deeds of heroism.

Connachar had almost given up hope when he remembered his best magician, Duanan Gacha Druid. "You are supposed to be the most powerful magician in Ireland," the king said. "I have spent sacks of gold on books of spells for you and on ingredients for your magic potions, yet still my enemies escape from me. What can you do?"

"I will find a way to stop them," replied the wizard, lifting up his arms and pointing towards the middle distance. Suddenly a vast, dense forest appeared, with trees, briars, and underbrush blocking the way of the sons of Uisnech. But Naois and Allen and Arden hacked their way through the middle of the trees, and Deirdre followed, holding Naois' hand.

"It's hopeless," said Connachar. "They can get through the trees with hardly a moment's hesitation. Surely we are powerless to stop them escaping."

"Then I will find another way to stop them," proclaimed the magician, lifting his arms once more. This time, instead of a grass-covered plain in front of the sons of Uisnech, there was a grey sea. But Naois and Allen and Arden took off their outer clothes and each man tied them in a bundle on his back. Naois lifted Deirdre and put her on his shoulders.

Then the three men began to wade steadily through the great grey sea, walking further and further away from Connachar.

"They are still getting away," moaned the king. "Have you no other powers to stop them in their tracks?"

"I have yet one more way to stop them," cried the druid, gesturing with his arms yet again. And no sooner had the druid raised his arms than the sea began to freeze. Each wave was as sharp as a sword on one side, and the other side was coated with deadly poison. It seemed that no living thing would be able to pass through.

Arden was the first to be overcome. Naois lifted him above the frozen waves, but Arden was already dying. Soon Allen too was feeling faint, and perished before Naois could do anything to help him. When he saw his two beloved brothers dead beside him, Naois too gave up hope. With his brothers gone he little cared whether he was alive or dead, and soon he was overcome by the deadly frozen sea.

"All the sons of Uisnech are gone," said the druid. "You may take your rightful wife."

But hard as he looked, Connachar could no longer see Deirdre. "Take away the frozen waves, so that I can see if she still lives," commanded the king. The druid lifted his arms once more and his magic took away the frozen sea, and there was the green plain once more. In the centre were the three dead sons of Uisnech, and by their side was poor Deirdre,

her head bowed in mourning for the death of Naois, the man she truly loved with all her heart.

Connachar ordered graves to be dug for the three brothers, and Deirdre followed them, still sorrowing, to the burial place. When she arrived, she told the gravediggers to make the grave larger and wider, until she jumped into the grave beside the body of Naois, and died by his side.

The king told his men to take her body out of the grave and buried it well away, on the opposite shore of the loch. But as time went by, a fir tree grew above the grave of Naois, and another over Deirdre's grave. Slowly, the two trees grew together, until their branches met above the loch's waters. Connachar did not like to be reminded of the love of Naois and Deirdre, so ordered the branches to be cut. Again, the branches grew, and again they were removed. But the time came when Connachar took a new wife, and she told him to let the branches grow over the waters as they would, and to leave the dead to lie in peace.

Stuck for a Story

There was once a king of Leinster whose favourite pastime was listening to stories. Every evening, before the king went to sleep, he called his best story-teller to him, and the story-teller told him a story, a different one each night. And whatever problems or worries had troubled the king during the day, they were eased away by the skill of the story-teller, and the king always had a good night's sleep. In return, the king granted his story-teller a large estate, with a big house and acres of land, for he thought that the story-teller was one of the most important men in his entire kingdom.

Each morning, when the story-teller got up, he went for a walk

around his estate before breakfast and thought up his story for the evening. But one morning, after walking around his whole estate, he found it impossible to think of a new tale. He seemed to be unable to get beyond "There was once a king of Ireland" or "In olden times there was a great king with three sons".

His wife called the story-teller in to breakfast, but he said he would not come in until he had thought of a story. Then, as she was calling him again, he saw an old, lame beggarman in the distance, and went up to talk to him.

"Good morning to you. Who might you be, and what are you doing here?" asked the story-teller.

"Never mind who I am," replied the old man. "I was resting awhile, for my leg is painful and I am tired, wondering who would play a game of dice with me."

The story-teller thought that a poor old man would have little money to gamble with. But the beggar said he had a hundred gold pieces, and the story-teller's wife said, "Why don't you play with him? A story might come to you afterwards." And so the two men began to throw.

Things did not go well for the story-teller. Soon he had lost all his money, but the old man still asked him to play another game. "I have no money left," said the story-teller.

"Then play for your chariot and horses and hounds," said the old man. The story-teller was unwilling to gamble away his possessions, but his wife encouraged him to take the risk.

"Go on, play another game, you might win. And anyway I don't mind walking." So they threw the dice, and again the story-teller lost the game.

"Will you play again," said the old man.

"Don't make fun of me," said the story-teller. "I have nothing to stake."

"Then play for your wife," said the beggar. Once again, the story-teller was unwilling, and turned his back on the beggar, but again his wife encouraged him, so they played and the story-teller lost once more.

The story-teller's wife went to join the beggar.

"Have you anything else to stake?" asked the old man. When the story-teller remained silent, the old man said simply, "Stake yourself."

They rolled the dice for the final time, and yet again the story-teller was the loser. "You have won me," said the storyteller. "Now what will you do with me?"

"What kind of animal would you prefer to be, a fox, a deer, or a hare?"

The story-teller thought, and decided that he would rather be a hare, for at least he would be able to run away from danger. So the old man took a wand out of his pocket and turned the story-teller into a hare. Then his wife called her hounds, and they chased the hare, round and

round the field, and all along the high stone wall that ran around it. And all the while the beggar and the story-teller's wife laughed and laughed to see the hare twist, turn, and double back on his path to try to avoid the hounds. The hare tried to hide behind the wife, but she kicked him back into the field. The hounds were about to catch him when the beggar waved his wand and the story-teller reappeared in the hare's place.

When the beggar asked the story-teller how he liked the hunt, the story-teller said he wished he was a hundred miles away. Suddenly, the beggar waved his wand, and the story-teller found himself in a different part of the country, at the castle of the lord Hugh O'Donnell. What was more, the story-teller realised quickly that he was invisible – he could see all about him, but no-one could see him.

Soon the beggar arrived at O'Donnell's castle.

"Where have you come from and what do you do?" asked the lord.

"I am a great traveller and magician," said the beggar.

Soon, the beggar was playing tricks on O'Donnell's men. "Give me six pieces of silver and I will show you that I can move one of my ears without moving the other."

"Done," said one of O'Donnell's men. "You'll never move one ear without moving the other, even great ears like yours!"

The beggarman then put one hand to one of his ears, and gave it a sharp pull.

O'Donnell roared with laughter, and paid the beggar six pieces of silver for the joke. But his man was less pleased. "What sort of trick do you call that?" he said. "Any fool could move his ear that way." And the man gave his own ear a mighty pull – and off came ear and head together.

Everyone was dumbstruck, except for the beggar, who said, "Now I'll show you an even better trick." He took out of his bag a ball of silk, unrolled it, and threw it up into the air, where it turned into a thick rope. Then he sent a hare racing up the rope, followed by a hound to chase it.

"Who will catch the hound and stop it eating my hare?" challenged the beggar. Sure enough, one of O'Donnell's men ran up the rope, and everyone below waited. When nothing had happened for a while, the beggar said, "It looks as if he has fallen asleep and let the dog eat the hare."

The beggar began to wind up the rope, and sure enough, there was the man fast asleep and the hound polishing off the hare. The old beggar looked angry that the man had failed in his task, drew his sword, and beheaded both man and hound.

O'Donnell was enraged that two of his men, and one of his best hounds, had been beheaded in his own castle. He went to seize the beggar, but the old man put up his hand. "Give me ten pieces of silver for each of them, and they shall be cured."

No sooner had O'Donnell paid over the silver, than men and hound were restored to their former health. As for the beggar, he had vanished, taking the invisible story-teller with him.

To the story-teller's relief he found himself back at the court of the King of Leinster, with the beggar beside him. But his relief did not last long. The king was looking for his story-teller, and instead here was the old beggar, who started to insult the royal harpers. "Their noise is worse than a cat purring over its food, or buzzing honey-bees," said the beggar.

"Hang the man who insults my harpers," shouted the king. But when the king's guards took him off to be hanged, the beggar escaped, and they found that the king's favourite brother was mysteriously hanged in his place.

"Hang the right man this time!" bawled the king. But this time the king's best harper was found on the gibbet. "Do you want to try hanging me again?" grinned the beggar. "Get out!" roared the king.

But before he went, the beggar made the story-teller visible again, and gave him back his chariot, his horses, his hounds – and his wife. "I had heard you were in difficulties," he said to the story-teller. "Now you have the story of your adventures to tell the king." Sure enough, the king thought the new story was the best he had ever heard. From that day on, it was the tale the king always wanted to hear, and the story-teller never had to think up a new story again.

The Legend of Knockgrafton

By the Galtee mountains long ago lived a poor basket-maker. He always wore a sprig of foxglove in his straw hat, so everyone called him Lusmore, an old Irish name for the foxglove. The most noticeable thing about Lusmore was that he had a huge hump on his back. This hump was so large that his head pressed down and his chin rested on his chest.

When they first saw Lusmore, most people were scared of him. But when they got to know him, they realised that he was one of the most charming and helpful of people. People were surprised that he was so sweet-tempered, since he had to bear such a deformity.

One day, Lusmore had been to a nearby town to sell some baskets, and he was walking back home. He could only go quite slowly, and found himself by the ancient mound at Knockgrafton as it got dark. He still had a way to travel, so decided to sit down beside the mound and rest for a while.

As soon as he sat down, Lusmore began to hear the most beautiful, unearthly music. He had never heard anything so melodious before, with many voices singing different words, but blending in perfect harmony. Stranger still, the sound seemed to be coming from within the mound.

Lusmore was enchanted with the music which came from the mound, and eventually started to sing along with it, adding his own strain which

blended beautifully with the music, making it sound even better than before. Suddenly, Lusmore found himself picked up at lightning speed, and before he knew what had happened, he was inside the mound. All around Lusmore danced tiny fairies, obviously delighted that he had liked their singing and added his own voice to their song. Round and round they danced, in constant movement in time to the melodious song, and Lusmore smiled in amazement and enjoyment.

When the song was finally over, Lusmore watched the group of fairies start to talk among themselves, occasionally glancing up at him before going back to their conversation. He felt rather frightened, wondering what they would do to him now that he had seen inside their secret home. Then one fairy stepped out from the group and came towards him, chanting, "Lusmore, Lusmore, The hump that you bore, You shall have it no more, See it fall to the floor, Lusmore, Lusmore!"

Lusmore felt lighter, and he seemed to be able to move

more easily. In fact, he felt as if he could jump to the Moon and back. Slowly, he started to lift his head, and, yes, he could stand up straight, straighter than he had ever stood before. It was true! The hump was gone!

As he looked around him, noticing again the strange beauty of the fairies who had been so kind to him, Lusmore began to feel dizzy. Then a tiredness came upon him and he fell asleep amongst the fairies.

When Lusmore awoke, he found himself outside the mound at Knockgrafton, and the morning sun was shining brightly. He said his prayers, then moved his hand gingerly towards his back. There was still no hump, and Lusmore stood proudly up, standing his full height for the first time. To his delight he also noticed that the fairies had left him dressed in a smart new suit of clothes. So off he went home, with a spring in his step that he had never had before.

To begin with, none of his neighbours recognised Lusmore. But when they realised that he had lost his hump, word spread quickly, and soon everyone was talking about Lusmore's amazing good fortune.

One day, Lusmore was sitting by his door working away at a new basket, when an old woman appeared.

"Good day," she said. "I am looking for a man called Lusmore, who had his hump removed by the fairies. For my best friend's son has such a hump, and if he could visit the fairies just as Lusmore did, perhaps he too could be cured."

The basket-maker told the old woman that she had found Lusmore, and explained the story of how he had heard the fairies singing, how he had joined in their song, how his hump had been taken away, and how he had been given a new suit of clothes. And the old woman thanked Lusmore, and went back to tell her friend what her son, Jack Madden, should do to rid himself of his hump.

Jack Madden set off for the old mound at Knockgrafton,

and sat down beside it. Soon he began to hear the bewitching sound of the fairies singing. In fact, the music was even sweeter than before, because the fairies had added Lusmore's part to their song. Jack Madden was in a hurry to be rid of his hump, and started joining in straightaway. Unlike Lusmore, he was a greedy fellow, who thought that if he sung louder, he might get two new suits of clothes instead of Lusmore's one. And unlike Lusmore, Jack did not listen carefully to the song, and make his own voice blend with the fairies. He bawled away as loudly as he could, almost shouting out the fairies in his eagerness to be heard.

Just as he expected, Jack Madden was taken inside the mound and surrounded by fairies. But the fairies were angry with Jack Madden. "Who was spoiling our song?" they cried. And one of the fairies started to chant at Jack Madden.

"Jack Madden, Jack Madden, You are such a bad'un, Your life we will sadden, Two humps for Jack Madden!"

And a group of fairies took Lusmore's old hump and stuck it on Jack's back.

When Jack Madden's mother and her friend came to the mound to look for Jack, they found him with his two humps. Although they pulled and pulled at the new hump, they could not remove it. They went home cursing the fairies and anyone who dared to go and listen to fairy music. And poor Jack Madden had two humps for the rest of his life.

A Donegal Fairy

There was once an old woman who lived in Donegal, and she was boiling a large pot of water over the fire. The water was just starting to boil when suddenly, one of the little people slid down the chimney and fell with one leg in the hot water.

He screamed a piercing scream, and the old lady looked on in wonder as dozens of tiny fairies quickly appeared around the fireplace and pulled him out of the water.

One of the rescuers pointed suspiciously towards the old woman. "Did the old wife scald you?" said the tiny figure, with a menacing tone in his voice.

"No, no, it was my own fault. I scalded myself," replied the first fairy.

"Ah, just as well for her," said the rescuer. "If she had scalded you, we would have made her squeal."

The Giant's Causeway

In ancient times, when giants lived in Ireland, there were two who were the strongest and most famous giants of them all, Fin M'Coul and Cucullin. Cucullin rampaged all over Ireland, fighting with every giant he met, and always coming out the winner. People said that Cucullin could make an earthquake by stamping on the ground, and that he once flattened a thunderbolt into a pancake, and carried it around in his pocket. They said that his strength lay in the middle finger of his right hand. Fin was strong too, but he was secretly afraid of Cucullin, and whenever he heard that the other giant was coming near, Fin found some excuse to move on.

It happened at one time that Fin and his relatives were away working on the Giant's Causeway, a great road that they were building over the sea to link Ireland and Scotland. As they worked, word reached Fin that Cucullin was on his way. "I think I'll be off home for a while to see my wife Oonagh," said Fin. "She misses me when I go away to work."

So Fin set off to his home on top of the hill at Knockmany. Many people wondered why Fin and Oonagh lived there. It was a long climb up and they had to carry their water to the top. Fin said he chose the place because he liked the view. In truth, he lived there so that he could see whether Cucullin was coming. And Knockmany was the best lookout for miles around, higher than any hill in the region except for the nearby hill of Cullamore, where Oonagh's sister Granua lived.

As Fin embraced Oonagh, she asked him, "What brought you home so early, Fin?"

"I came home to see you, my love," said Fin, and the couple went in happily to eat.

Oonagh had not been long with her husband when she realised that he was worried, and she guessed that there was some other reason for his return.

"It's this Cucullin that's troubling me," admitted Fin. "He can make the earth shake by stamping his foot, and he can squash thunderbolts into pancakes. The beast is coming. If I run away, I will be disgraced; if I stay, he'll squash me like a pancake. I don't know what I'm going to do."

"Well, don't despair," said his wife. "Maybe I can get you out of this scrape." And Fin wondered what she was going to do.

First of all, Oonagh called across to her sister Granua, on the neighbouring hill of Cullamore. "Sister, what can you see?" she shouted.

"I can see the greatest giant I ever saw. He is coming this way and has just walked through Dungannon. I will call him and offer him a drink. That may give you and Fin some more time to prepare for him."

Meanwhile, Fin was getting more and more nervous. All he could think of was the thunderbolt, flattened like a pancake in Cucullin's pocket, and he trembled with fear at what might become of them.

"Be easy, Fin," said Oonagh. "Your talk of pancakes has given me an idea. I am going to bake some bread."

"What's the point of baking bread at a time like this?" wailed Fin. But Oonagh ignored him, and started mixing the dough, singing quietly to herself, as if she had not a care in the world. She then went out to visit her neighbours, something that made Fin even more anxious. She did not seem to be giving a thought to the giant Cucullin.

When Oonagh returned, she was carrying twenty-one iron griddles, which she had borrowed from her neighbours. She went back to her work and kneaded each iron griddle into a portion of the dough, to make twenty-one bread cakes, each with a hard iron griddle in the centre. Oonagh baked the bread cakes in the fire, and put them away in her cupboard when they were done. Then she sat down to rest, and smiled contentedly.

On the following day, they finally spied Cucullin coming up the hill towards their house. "Jump into bed," said Oonagh to Fin. "You must pretend to be your own child. Don't say anything, but listen to what I say, and be guided by me."

At two o'clock, as they expected, Cucullin arrived. "Is this the house of Fin M'Coul?" he asked. "I have heard talk that he says he is the strongest giant in all Ireland, but I want to put him to the test."

"Yes, this is his house, but he is not here. He left suddenly in great anger because someone told him that a great beast of a giant called Cucullin was in the neighbourhood, and he set out at once to catch him. I hope he doesn't catch the poor wretch, for if he does, Fin will surely knock the stuffing out of him."

"Well I am that Cucullin," replied the giant. "And I have been searching for him. He will be sorry when I find him, for I shall squash him like a pancake."

Fin began to tremble when he heard the dreaded word "pancake", but Oonagh simply laughed.

"You can't have seen Fin," she said. "For if you had, you would think differently. But since you are here, perhaps you could help me. You'll notice that the wind is blowing at the door and making a terrible draught. Turn the house round for me, as Fin would have done if he were here."

Cucullin could hardly believe that Fin had the strength to turn the whole house around. But he went outside, grasped the building in his hand, pulled hard, and moved it around, so that the wind no longer blew at the door.

"Now, Fin was telling me that he was going to crack those cliffs on the hill down below, to make a spring come up and bring us water.

Will you do that for me, since Fin is not here to do it himself?" Again, Cucullin was astonished at Fin's strength, and went outside to make a crack in the rocks for the water to come through.

Oonagh thanked him for the trouble he had taken, and offered him some food for his pains. And out with the meat and cabbage, she brought one of the bread cakes she had baked. When Cucullin bit on the bread, he cried out in pain, "Aagh! That's two of my best teeth broken!" he wailed. "But that's the only bread that my husband will eat," said Oonagh. "Try another cake. It may not be so hard." The hungry giant grabbed another, but his hand flew to his mouth in horror: "The Devil take your bread, or I'll have no teeth left!" he roared. Oonagh pretended to be surprised. "Even our son eats this bread," she said, passing Fin a bread cake with no iron inside.

By now Cucullin was shaking in terror. If the young lad was so strong he could eat bread like this, what would his father be like? Cucullin decided he would be off before Fin came home. But he could not resist asking to look at the child's teeth that could eat bread with iron inside.

"It's the back teeth that are the strongest," said Oonagh. "Put your finger into the child's mouth, and feel for yourself."

Cucullin slipped his middle finger into Fin's mouth, and Fin knew his chance had come. Fin bit hard on the giant's finger, and when Cucullin pulled his hand away in surprise, the middle finger was gone. Cucullin was crushed. He knew his strength was gone with his finger, and he ran from the house, screaming and roaring, and they never saw him again.

Fair, Brown, and Trembling

Once upon a time long ago lived King Hugh Curucha, and he had three daughters called Fair, Brown, and Trembling. Fair and Brown were his favourite daughters. They were always given new dresses and were allowed to go to church every Sunday. But Trembling, who was the most beautiful of the three, had to stay at home, where she did the cooking and housework. The other two forced Trembling to stay at home like this because they were jealous of her beauty, and feared that she might attract a husband before them.

After Trembling had been kept at home like this for seven years, the Prince of Emania met Fair, the eldest of the sisters, and fell in love with her. Just after this had happened, Fair and Brown went off to church as usual and Trembling stayed at home to cook dinner. As she worked, she talked to the old Henwife, the woman who kept the chickens on the royal farm, who had called at the kitchen. "Why haven't you gone to church too?" asked the Henwife.

"I cannot go to church," replied Trembling. "All my clothes are in tatters. Besides, if I dared to go to church, my sisters would beat me for leaving the house."

"If you could have a new dress," said the Henwife, "what sort of dress would you choose?"

"I would like a dress as white as the snow, with a pair of bright green shoes to go with it," replied Trembling.

Then the Henwife put on her cloak, snipped a tiny piece of cloth from the dress Trembling was wearing, and asked for the most beautiful white dress, and a brand new pair of green shoes. Straight away, a long white dress appeared in the old woman's hands, and a pair of green shoes, and she gave them to Trembling, who put them on. Then the Henwife gave the girl a honey-bird to put on her shoulder, and led her to the door. There stood a fine white horse, with a saddle and bridle richly decorated with gold. "Off you go to church," said the Henwife. "But when you get there, do not go inside, be sure to stand just outside the church door. As soon as the people start to leave at the end of Mass, be ready to ride off as quickly as you can."

So Trembling rode to church, and stayed by the door as the old woman had told her. Even though she remained outside, many people within caught a glimpse of her, and began to wonder who she was. At the end of Mass, several people ran out to get a better look at her, but she turned her horse and galloped away at great speed, so no one could catch her.

As she entered the kitchen, Trembling began to worry that no one had

finished cooking dinner for her sisters. But she saw straight away that the Henwife had cooked the meal, and Trembling put on her old dress as quickly as she could.

When Fair and Brown returned, they were full of talk about the mysterious lady in white whom they had seen outside the church door. They demanded that their father buy them fine white dresses like the lady's, and next Sunday, they wore their new dresses to church.

Again, the Henwife appeared in the kitchen, and asked Trembling if she wanted to go to church. This time the old woman produced a black satin dress, with red shoes for Trembling's feet. With the honey-bird on her shoulder, she rode on a black mare with a silver saddle, and stayed quietly by the door of the church.

The people in the church were even more amazed when they saw the strange lady by the door. Everyone wondered who she could be, but Trembling gave them no chance to find out, and rode away as soon as Mass was over.

Back home, Trembling removed her fine robe as she had before, and put the finishing touches to the meal prepared by the Henwife. When Fair and Brown arrived home from church, they were full of talk about the fine lady and her black satin dress. "No one even noticed our fine

dresses," complained Fair. "They were too busy admiring the lady by the church door and wondering who she might be. Everyone was staring at her with their mouths open, and none of the men even glanced at us!"

Fair and Brown would give their father no peace until he bought them fine black satin dresses, just like the one they had seen their sister wearing, and red shoes to go with them. Of course, Fair and Brown's dresses were not as elegant nor as finely made as Trembling's gown. They could not find one to match it anywhere in Ireland.

Off went Fair and Brown next Sunday in their new black dresses, and yet again the Henwife turned to Trembling and asked her what she wanted to wear to church. "I would dearly like a rose-red dress, a green cape, a hat with feathers of red, white and green, and shoes of the same colours."

The Henwife smiled to think of the fantastic mixture of colours that Trembling had chosen, but once more did her magic, and quickly Trembling was dressed in the garments of her choice, and mounted on a mare with diamond-shaped spots of white, blue, and gold over her body. The honey-bird began to sing as Trembling rode off to church, to wait outside the door.

By this time, news had spread all

over Ireland about the beautiful lady who waited outside the church every Sunday, and many lords and princes had come to see her for themselves. Amongst them was the Prince of Emania, who, once he had seen Trembling, forgot all about her elder sister, and vowed to catch the strange lady before she could ride away. At the end of Mass, the prince sprinted out of church, and ran behind Trembling's mare. He was just able to grab hold of one of her shoes, before she galloped away into the distance.

The Prince of Emania vowed that he would search the length and breadth of Ireland until he found the woman whose foot would fit the shoe in his hand. The other princes joined him, as they too were curious, and they searched in every town and village until they came to the house of Fair, Brown, and Trembling. Both Fair and Brown tried to force their feet into the shoe, but it was too small for them. The prince asked if there was any other woman in the house. Trembling began to speak up, but Fair and Brown tried to stop her.

"Oh, she is just a serving girl we keep to clean the house," said Fair. But the prince insisted that every woman should have the chance to try on the shoe.

When the shoe fitted exactly the prince was overjoyed. He was about to declare his love, when Trembling begged him to wait. She ran to the house of the Henwife, who helped her on with the white dress; then she returned home to show everyone that she was truly the mysterious lady. She then did the same thing with the other dresses, amazing her sisters more and more each time. The princes were just as surprised, and before she had put on the third dress, they were all challenging the Prince of Emania to fight for her hand.

The Prince of Emania fought bravely, defeating the Prince of Lochlin, who fought him for nine hours, the Prince of Spain, who fought for eight hours, and the Prince of Greece, who fought for seven hours. And at the end no one would fight the Prince of Emania, for they knew he would be the winner. So the

Prince of Emania married Trembling, and the celebrations lasted for a year and a day.

All seemed to be going happily, but Fair was still very jealous of her sister. So one day, she called on her sister, and the two walked by the coast. When they came to the sea, Fair waited until there was no-one to see her, then pushed Trembling into the water. Just as it seemed Trembling would drown, a great whale came and swallowed her up. When Fair returned to the prince she put on her sister's clothes and pretended to be Trembling. But even though the two were as alike as could be, the Prince was not fooled by her trick.

Now Fair thought that no one had seen her push her sister into the sea, but a young cow-boy had watched the two sisters from a nearby field. Next day he was again in the field when he saw the whale swim by and throw Trembling out upon the sand.

Then Trembling spoke to the cow-boy, saying "Run home and tell the prince my husband what has happened. If he does not come and shoot the whale, it will carry on swallowing me, and casting me out, while keeping me under a spell. I will never be able to leave the beach and come home."

The cow-boy ran to tell the Prince what had happened, but the elder sister stopped him in his tracks, and gave him a potion to drink. The drink made him forgetful, and he said nothing about what he had seen. The next day the cow-boy returned to the sea, and once more saw the whale cast out Trembling on the shore. Trembling asked the boy if he had taken her message to the Prince and the boy admitted that he had forgotten. Shamefully, he ran to tell the prince, and again Fair gave him the potion. On the third day, when the cow-boy was by the sea and saw Trembling cast out yet again, the girl guessed what had happened and spoke to him, saying "Do not let her give you any drink when you go home. She is using a potion to make you forget what has happened."

And so it was that the prince was finally brought news of his wife. He ran to the shore, loaded his gun, and shot the whale, releasing Trembling from the creature's spell. From then on the cow-boy lived in the Prince's household, and when he came of age, he married Trembling's daughter. They all lived happily, for many years, until the Prince and Trembling died, contented, of old age.

The Haughty Princess

There was once a king who had a daughter. She was very beautiful and many dukes, earls, princes, and even kings came from all around to ask for her hand in marriage. But the princess was a proud, haughty creature who would have none of them. As each suitor approached her, she would find fault with him, and send him packing, usually with a rude remark which meant that the suitor was sure to have nothing more to do with her.

One of her suitors was plump, and to him she said, "I shall not marry you, Beer Belly." Another had a pale face, and to him she said, "I shall not marry you, Death-Mask." A third suitor was tall and thin, and to him she said, "I shall not marry you, Ramrod." Yet another prince had a red complexion, and to him she said, "I shall not marry you, Beetroot." And so it went on, until every unmarried duke and earl and prince, and even king, for miles around had been rejected, and her father thought she would never find a man she liked.

Then one day a prince arrived who was so handsome, and so polite, that she found it hard to find any fault with him at all. But still the princess's pride got the better of her, and in the end, she looked at the brown curling hairs under his chin and said, somewhat reluctantly, "I shall not marry you, Whiskers".

The poor king was at his wit's end with his daughter, and finally lost his temper with her. "I'm sick of your rudeness. Soon no one will come to visit me for fear of what you will say to them. I shall give you to the first beggar who calls at our door for alms, and good riddance to you!"

Soon a poor beggar knocked at the door. His clothes were tattered and torn, his hair dirty and matted, and his beard long and straggling. Sure enough, the king called for the priest, and married his daughter to the bearded beggar. She cried and screamed and tried to run away, but there was nothing for it.

After the ceremony, the beggar led his bride off into a wood. When she asked where they were going, he told her that the wood and all the land around belonged to the king she had called Whiskers. The princess was even sadder that she had rejected the handsome king, and hung

her head in shame when she saw the poor, tumble-down shack where the beggar lived. The place was dirty and untidy, and there was no fire burning in the grate. So the princess had to put on a plain cotton dress, help her husband make the fire, clean the place, and prepare them a meal.

Meanwhile, the beggar gathered some twigs of willow, and after they had eaten, the two sat together making baskets. But the twigs bruised the princess's fingers, and she cried out with the pain. The beggar was not a cruel man, and saw that he must find some other work for her to do, so he gave her some cloth and thread, and set her to sewing. But although the princess tried hard, the needle made her fingers bleed, and again tears came to her eyes. So the beggar bought a basket full of cheap earthenware pots and sent her to market to sell them.

The princess did well at market on the first day, and returned with a profit. But the next morning, just after she had set out her wares, a drunken huntsman came riding through the market place, and his mount kicked its way through all the princess's pots. She returned to her husband in tears.

In the end, the beggar spoke to the cook at the palace of King Whiskers, and persuaded her to give his wife a job as a kitchen maid. The princess worked hard, and every day the cook gave her leftovers from the table to take home for her husband. The princess liked the cook, and got on quite well in the kitchen, but she was still sorry she had rejected King Whiskers.

A while later, the palace suddenly got busier. It turned out that King Whiskers was getting married. "Who is going to marry the king?" asked the princess. But no one knew who the bride was going to be.

Because they were curious, the princess and the cook decided to go and see what was going on in the great hall of the palace. Perhaps they would be able to see the mysterious bride. The princess opened the door quietly and the two of them peeped in.

King Whiskers himself was in the room, and strode over when he saw the door begin to open. "Spying on the king?" he said, looking hard at the princess. "You must pay for your nosiness by dancing a jig with me." The king took her hand, led her into the room, and all the musicians began to play. But as they whirled around, puddings and portions of meat began to fly out of her pockets, and everyone in the room roared with laughter. The princess began to run to the door, but the king caught her by the hand and took her to one side.

"Do you not realise who I am?" he asked her, smiling kindly. "I am King Whiskers, and your husband the beggar, and the drunken huntsman who broke your pots in the market place. Your father knew who I was when he let me marry you, and we arranged all this to rid you of your pride."

The princess was so confused she did not know what to say or do. All sorts of emotions, from joy to embarrassment, welled up inside her, but the strongest of all these feelings was love for her husband, King Whiskers. She laid her head on his shoulder, and began to cry.

When she had recovered, some of the palace maids led her away and helped her put on a fine dress fit for a queen. She went back to join her husband, and none of the guests realised that the new queen was the poor kitchen maid who had danced a jig with the king.

The Man Who Never Knew Fear

There were once two brothers, called Lawrence and Carrol. Lawrence was known as the bravest boy in the village and nothing made him afraid. Carrol, on the other hand, was fearful of the least thing, and would not even go out at night.

When their mother died, they had to decide who would watch her grave. In those days it was the tradition that when a person had died, their relatives would take it in turns to stand guard over the grave, to protect it from robbers.

Carrol, who did not want to watch his mother's grave at night, made a bet with his brother. "You say that nothing makes you afraid, but I bet you will not watch our mother's tomb tonight."

Lawrence replied, "I have the courage to stay there all night." He put on his sword and marched boldly to the graveyard, where he sat down on a gravestone next to his mother's tomb.

At first, all went well, but as the night went on, the young man became drowsy. He was almost dropping off to sleep, when he saw the most awesome sight. A huge black head was coming towards him. It seemed to float through the air, and Lawrence realised that there was no body attached to it. Without taking his eye from the head, Lawrence quickly drew his sword and held it out in front of him, ready to strike if the thing came any closer. But it did not, and Lawrence stayed, looking straight at the head, until dawn.

When he got home, Lawrence told Carrol what he had seen. "Were you afraid?" asked Carrol.

"Of course I wasn't," replied Lawrence. "You know that nothing in the world will frighten me."

"I bet you will not watch another night," taunted Carrol.

"I would, but I have lost a whole night's sleep. You go tonight, and I will watch the third night."

But Carrol said no, so Lawrence slept in the afternoon, and went off to the graveyard at dusk. Around midnight, a huge black monster appeared and started to scratch near his mother's grave. Lawrence drew his sword and chopped the monster up. The graveyard was peaceful until daybreak.

Carrol was waiting for his brother to come home. "Did the great head appear before you again?" he asked.

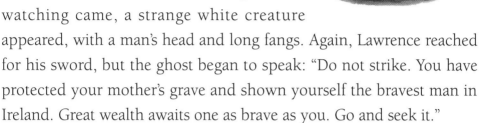

"No, but a monster came and tried to dig up mother's body," said Lawrence.

When the third and final night of watching came, a strange white creature appeared, with a man's head and long fangs. Again, Lawrence reached for his sword, but the ghost began to speak: "Do not strike. You have protected your mother's grave and shown yourself the bravest man in Ireland. Great wealth awaits one as brave as you. Go and seek it."

The next day Lawrence took the fifty pounds he had won from his brother in the bet, and set out to seek his riches. On his way he met a baker, and told him the story of his adventures in the graveyard. "I'll bet you another fifty pounds you'll be scared by the graveyard near here," said the baker. "Go there tonight, and bring me the goblet on the altar of the old church." The baker had heard that the church was haunted, and that no one ever came out of the building alive.

In the dead of night, Lawrence strode up to the door of the church and hit it firmly with his sword. Straight out of the door charged an

 enormous black ram, with horns as long and sharp as scythes. In a flash, Lawrence struck out at the creature, and it fled, scattering its blood all around the church doorway. Then Lawrence took the goblet, and went to the baker.

The baker was astounded that Lawrence had returned in one piece, and they went to see the priest to tell him the news. The priest was overcome with joy. He paid the young man still more money, and straight away prepared to say Mass in the church. And Lawrence continued his journey, searching for something that would make him afraid.

Lawrence travelled a long way through lonely countryside, and hardly saw a house all day, when he came to a valley where a crowd of people were gathered. They were watching two men playing a ball game, but they seemed to be frightened. Suddenly, one of the players hurled the ball towards Lawrence, and it hit him straight in the chest. Lawrence reached to catch it, and saw that it was the head of a man. As Lawrence took hold of it, the head screeched, "Are you not afraid?"

"No I am not!" said Lawrence, and straight away the head, and the crowd of people, vanished from sight.

Lawrence carried on until he came to a town, by which time he was weary and in need of lodgings. When he explained his quest to a young man, his acquaintance pointed to a large house across the road. "If you will stay the night in there, you will find something to put fear in you. If you can stand it, I will give you fifty pounds more."

So Lawrence found himself making his lodgings inside a cold, dark cellar, waiting to see what would happen. The first night, a bull and a stallion came into the room with a fearful neighing and bellowing, and began to fight for all they were worth. The next night two great black rams fought in the room, with such screeching and howling that

Lawrence thought they would wake the whole town. But still he did not feel fear.

On his third night in the old house the ghost of an old, grey man appeared. "You are truly the bravest man in Ireland," he said. "Never, since I died twenty years ago, have I found such a hero as you. Do one thing for me, and I will lead you to your riches." The old man went on to tell Lawrence how he had once wronged an old woman called Mary Kerrigan, and how he wanted Lawrence to go to Mary and beg her forgiveness. If he did this he could buy the old house and marry the old man's daughter.

Lawrence went to Mary Kerrigan and won her forgiveness. He bought the house, and all the land around it, and married the old man's daughter. They lived happily in the house, and the ghosts never returned.

The Enchantment of Earl Gerald

Earl Gerald was one of the bravest leaders in Ireland long ago. He lived in a castle at Mullaghmast with his lady and his knights, and whenever Ireland was attacked, Earl Gerald was among the first to join the fight to defend his homeland.

As well as being a great fighter, Gerald was also a magician who could change himself into any shape or form that he wanted. His wife was fascinated by this, but had never seen Gerald change his shape, although she had often asked him to show her how he could transform himself into the shape of some strange beast. Gerald always put her off with some excuse, until one day her pleading got too much for him.

"Very well," said Earl Gerald. "I will do what you ask. But you must promise not to show any fear when I change my shape. If you are frightened, I will not be able to change myself back again for hundreds of years."

She protested that the wife of such a noble warrior, who had seen him ride into battle against fearsome enemies, would not be frightened by such a small thing, so Gerald agreed to change his shape.

They were sitting quietly in the great chamber of the castle when suddenly Gerald vanished and a beautiful goldfinch was flying around the room. His wife was shocked by the sudden change, but

did her best to stay calm and keep her side of the bargain. All went well, and she watched the little bird fly out into the garden, return, and perch in her lap. Gerald's wife was delighted with the bird, and smiled merrily, when suddenly and without warning, a great hawk swooped through the open windows, diving towards the finch. The lady screamed, even though the hawk missed Gerald and crashed into the table top, where its sharp beak stuck into the wood.

The damage was done. Gerald's wife had shown her fear. As she looked down to where the goldfinch had perched, she realised that the tiny bird had vanished. She never saw either the goldfinch or Earl Gerald again.

Many hundreds of years have passed by since Earl Gerald disappeared, and his poor wife is long dead. But occasionally, Gerald may be seen. Once in seven years, he mounts his steed and is seen riding around the Curragh of Kildare. Those few who have glimpsed him say that his horse has shoes made of silver, and the story goes that when these shoes are finally worn away, Gerald will return, fight a great battle, and rule as King of Ireland for forty years.

Meanwhile, in a great cavern beneath the old castle of Mullaghmast, Gerald and his knights sleep their long sleep. They are dressed in full armour and sit around a long table with the Earl at the head. Their horses, saddled and bridled, stand ready. When the right moment comes, a young lad with six fingers on each hand will blow a trumpet to awaken them.

Once, almost one hundred years ago, Earl Gerald was on one of his seven-yearly rides and an old horse-dealer was passing the cavern where Gerald's knights were still sleeping. There were lights in the cavern, and the horse-dealer went in to have a look. He was amazed to see the knights in their armour, all slumped on the table fast asleep, and the fine horses

waiting there. He was looking at their steeds, and thinking whether he might lead one of the beasts away to market, when he dropped the bridle he was holding. The clattering of the falling bridle echoed in the cavern and one of the knights stirred in his slumber.

"Has the time come?" groaned the knight, his voice husky with sleep. The horsedealer was struck dumb for a moment, as the knight's voice echoed in the cave. Finally he replied.

"No, the time has not come yet. But it soon will."

The knight slumped back on to the table, his helmet giving a heavy clank on the board. The horse-dealer ran away home with all the speed he could manage. And Earl Gerald's knights slept on.

The Story of the Little Bird

Once long ago in a monastery in Ireland there lived a holy man. He was walking one day in the garden of his monastery, when he decided to kneel down and pray, to give thanks to God for the beauty of all the flowers and plants and herbs around him. As he did so, he heard a small bird singing, and never before had he heard any song as sweet.

When his prayers, were finished, the monk stood up and listened to the bird, and when the creature flew away from the garden, singing as it went, he followed it.

In a while they came to a small grove of trees outside the monastery grounds, and there the bird continued its song. As the bird hopped from tree to tree, still singing all the while, the monk carried on following the little creature, until they had gone a great distance. The more the little bird sang, the more the monk was enchanted by the music it made.

Eventually, the two had travelled far away from the monastery, and the monk realised that it would soon be night-time. So reluctantly, he left the bird behind and retraced his steps, arriving back home as the sun was going down in the west. As the sun set, it lit up the sky with all the colours of the rainbow, and the monk thought that the sight was

almost as beautiful and heavenly as the song of the little bird he had been listening to all afternoon long.

But the glorious sunset was not the only sight that surprised the monk. As he entered the abbey gates, everything around him seemed changed from before. In the garden grew different plants, in the courtyard the brothers had different faces, and even the abbey buildings seemed to have altered. He knew he was in the right place, yet how could all these changes have taken place in a single afternoon?

The holy man walked across the courtyard and greeted the first monk he saw. "Brother, how is it that our abbey has changed so much since this morning? There are fresh plants in the garden, new faces amongst the brothers, and even the stones of the church seem different."

The second monk looked at the holy man carefully. "Why do you ask

these questions, brother? There have been no changes. Our church and gardens have not altered since morning, and we have no new brothers here – except for yourself, for though you wear the habit of our order, I have not seen you before." And the two monks looked at each other in wonder. Neither could understand what had happened.

When he saw that the brother was quite puzzled, the holy man started to tell his incredible story. He told his companion how he had gone to walk in the monastery garden, how he had heard the little bird, and how he had followed the creature far into the countryside to listen to its beautiful song.

As the holy man spoke, the expression on the second monk's face turned from puzzlement to

surprise. He said, "There is a story in our order about a brother like you who went missing one day after a bird was heard singing. He never returned to the abbey, and no one knew what befell him, and all this happened two hundred years ago."

The holy man looked at his companion and replied, "That is indeed my story. The time of my death has finally arrived. Praised be the Lord for his mercies to me." And the holy man begged the second monk to take his confession and give him absolution, for the hour of his death was near. All this was done, the holy man died before midnight, and he was buried with great solemnity in the abbey church.

Ever since, the monks of the abbey have told this story. They say that the little bird was an angel of the Lord, and that this was God's way of taking the soul of a man who was known for his holiness and his love of the beauties of nature.

The Demon Cat

In Connemara there lived a woman who was very fond of fish. She married a fisherman, and on most days he brought home a good catch. They had enough fish to sell in the market and plenty for the wife to eat. But every night a large black cat would break into their house and steal the best fish.

To begin with, the cat came only at night, and the woman could never catch it. But one day, dark storm clouds came, and the beast arrived during the daytime, as the woman and her friends were spinning. The woman's daughter looked at the cat. "That great beast must be the devil," she said. Straight away the cat scratched the girl's arm, and stood by the door to stop them escaping. "I'll teach you how to behave to a gentleman," he said.

The women began to scream, and a passing man heard them, and pushed at the door. The cat held the door closed, but the passer-by managed to get his stick through and gave the cat a hefty blow. The beast would have none of this, and jumped up to scratch the man's face. Blood flew everywhere, and the man ran off, scared out of his wits.

"Now I'll have my dinner," said the cat, once more taking the biggest fish. And when the women tried to hit it, it scratched and tore at them, and they ran away in terror.

When she had got her breath back, the fisherman's wife decided on a new plan. She went to the priest, asked for some holy water, and

returned home. Walking on tiptoe, she entered her house, and there was the cat, helping himself to more fish. Silently she sprinkled holy water on to the beast, and thick black smoke rose up from its fur. Soon the cat began to shrivel up, and only the animal's two red eyes could be seen, staring through the blackness. Then the animal's remains disappeared, and the smoke began to clear away. The woman knew that the demon cat would trouble her no more.

This edition is published by Armadillo
an imprint of Anness Publishing Limited
info@anness.com   www.annesspublishing.com

Illustrations © Sue Clarke, Anna Cynthia Leplar, Jacqueline Mair,
Sheila Moxley, and Jane Tattersfield
Introduction and retellings © Anness Publishing Limited
Volume © Anness Publishing Limited 2019

This edition: Publisher Joanna Lorenz and Editorial Director Helen Sudell
With thanks to Emma Bradford and Neil Philip of Albion Press,
who created this book.

Philip Wilson is the author of several books on religion and mythology, and is an
enthusiast for all kinds of traditional tales. His other books include *Celtic Fairytales*,
Welsh Fairytales, and *Scottish Fairytales*, all published by Armadillo.

Neil Philip is a writer, folklorist and poet. Among his many books are
The Little Mermaid and Other Tales by Hans Christian Andersen, *Folktales of Eastern Europe*,
Fairy Tales of the Brothers Grimm, and *Little Red Riding Hood and Other Fairy Tales
by Charles Perrault*, all published by Armadillo.